P9-DIY-431

Mama Elizabeti

by STEPHANIE STUVE-BODEEN

illustrated by CHRISTY HALE

LEE & LOW BOOKS, INC. *New York*

LEE & LOW BOOKS Inc., 95 Madison Avenue, New York, NY 10016
www.leeandlow.com

Printed in Hong Kong by South China Printing Co. (1988) Ltd.

Book design by Christy Hale
Book production by The Kids at Our House

The text is set in Octavian.
The illustrations are rendered in mixed media.

10 9 8 7 6 5 4 3 2 1
First Edition

Library of Congress Cataloging-in-Publication Data
Stuve-Bodeen, Stephanie.
Mama Elizabeti / by Stephanie Stuve-Bodeen ; illustrated by Christy Hale.—1st ed.
p. cm.
Summary: When her mother has a new baby, Elizabeti is given charge of her younger brother and finds it more difficult to take care of him than it was to care for her rock doll.
ISBN 1-58430-002-7
[1. Brothers and sisters—Fiction. 2. Babies—Fiction. 3. Tanzania—Fiction.]
I. Hale, Christy, ill. II. Title.
PZ7.S9418 Mam 2000
[E]—dc21 99-047890

For my parents, and all the creatures
who ever called Glennenn Farm home—S.S.-B.

For my mother-in-law, Barbara Gibney—C.H.

Elizabeti had a new baby sister named Flora. Mama had to take care of the baby, so it was time for Elizabeti to take care of her brother Obedi. Elizabeti knew just what to do. She had been taking care of her rock doll, Eva, since Obedi was a baby.

Elizabeti kissed Eva, set her gently in the corner, and went to get Obedi, who was having breakfast with Baba, their father.

Baba was leaving for work, and Elizabeti helped Obedi wave goodbye.

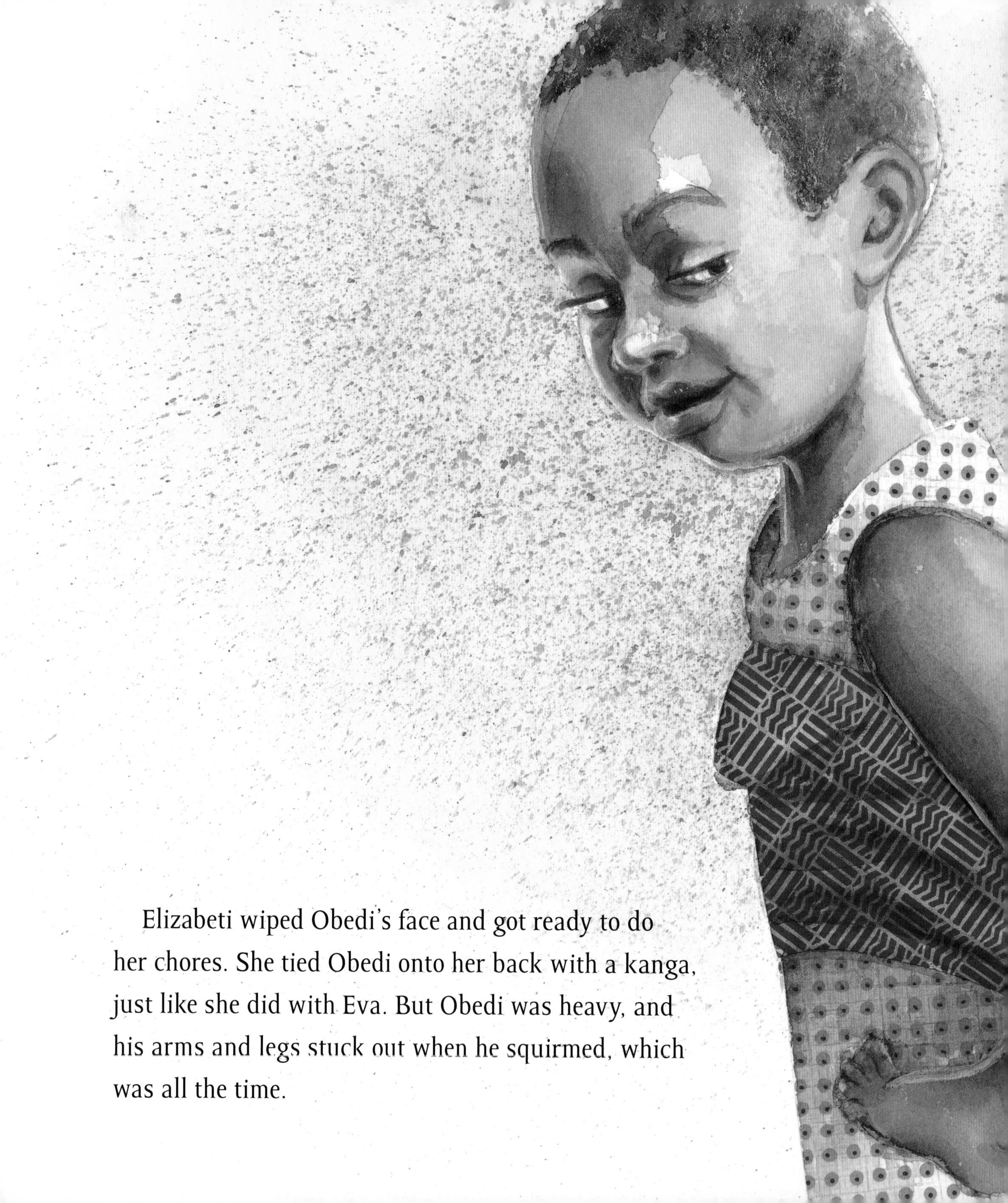

Elizabeti wiped Obedi's face and got ready to do her chores. She tied Obedi onto her back with a kanga, just like she did with Eva. But Obedi was heavy, and his arms and legs stuck out when he squirmed, which was all the time.

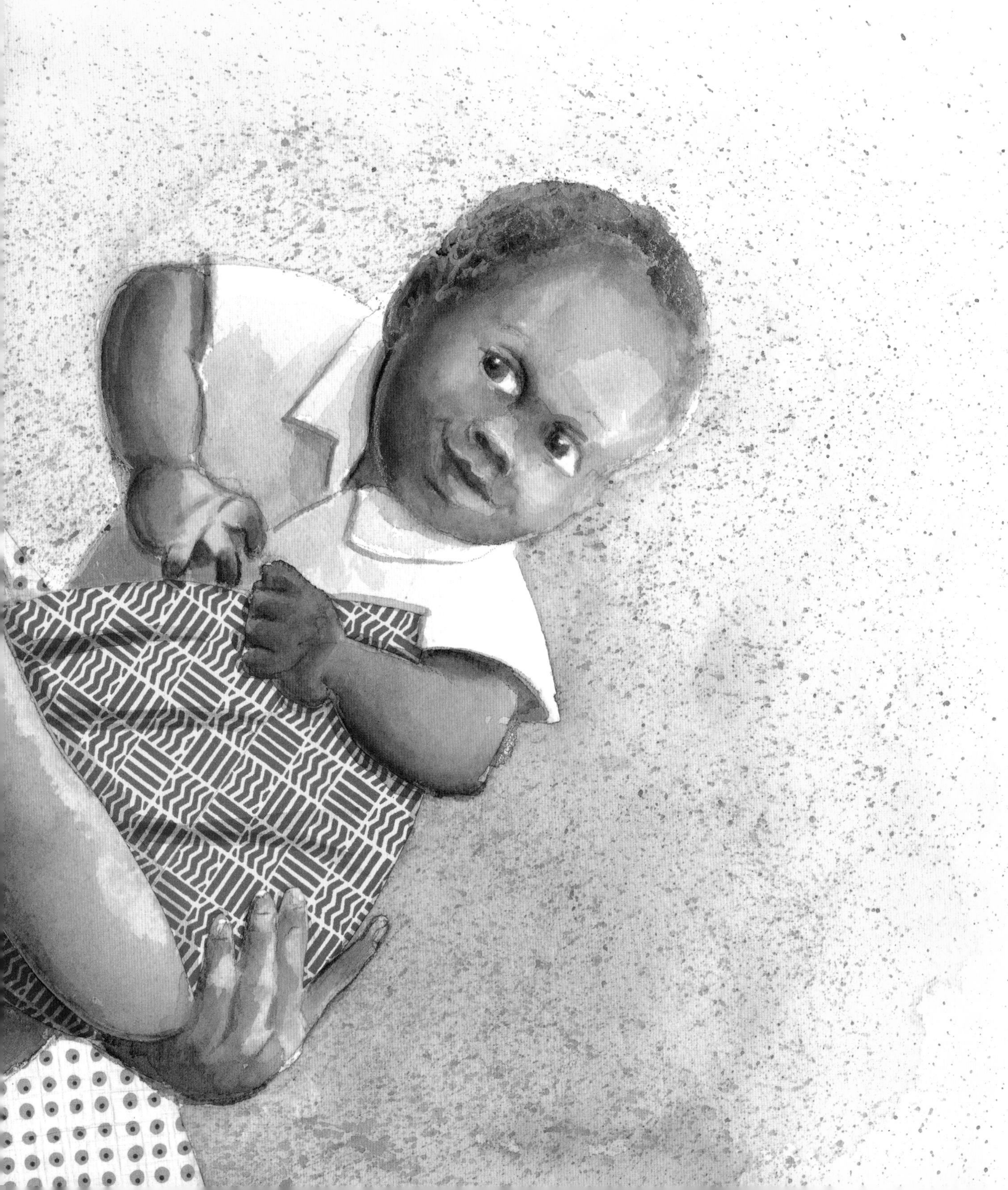

Elizabeti tried to sweep the floor, but Obedi pulled her hair.

Elizabeti sifted rocks out of the rice, but Obedi slapped at the basket, spilling some of the rice on the ground.

Elizabeti did the laundry, but when she turned around to hang it up, Obedi kicked the clean clothes into the dirt.

Elizabeti went to get water, but Obedi wiggled so much that the heavy water jug fell off Elizabeti's head.

Elizabeti slumped down near the fallen jug. How did Mama ever get anything done? Elizabeti wished she could just take care of Eva again. Eva never pulled her hair or spilled the rice or ruined the laundry.

Elizabeti sighed. She needed to find a way to carry Obedi and the water jug all the way home.

A woman walked by, but her head was piled high with bananas and she carried a baby on her back. She couldn't help Elizabeti.

Elizabeti smiled when she saw her friend Rahaili coming, carrying only a sack in her arms. But when Elizabeti peeked in the sack she saw a small pig. Rahaili was on her way to the market and couldn't help Elizabeti either.

Elizabeti spread the kanga on the ground and put Obedi on it, just like she always did with Eva. Elizabeti picked up the water jug and went to the well. She filled the jug and quickly returned.

But the kanga was empty!

Elizabeti set the water jug on the ground and began to look for Obedi. She called and called, but he didn't come.

Elizabeti knelt on the kanga and swallowed hard. What if she never found Obedi? Her eyes filled with tears when she thought about Mama and Baba. They would think she didn't know how to take care of a real baby.

All of a sudden, Elizabeti heard a squeal, and Obedi came out from behind a thorn tree. He was walking!

Elizabeti ran to Obedi and lifted him into her arms, holding on tightly. She felt his chubby arms around her neck, and she laughed when he gave her a loud, wet kiss. Eva had never done that!

Elizabeti picked up the kanga. She tied one end around Obedi's middle and the other around her own. Then Elizabeti picked up the water jug and started home. She stopped to pull Obedi up whenever he fell, but they made it back in time for dinner.

That night, Mama rocked Flora to sleep while Elizabeti rocked Obedi. She hoped he would fall asleep quickly so she could play with Eva.

Obedi snuggled his head under Elizabeti's chin. She smiled and put her face in his fuzzy hair. As Elizabeti rested her head on his, she saw Eva nestled in the corner. There would be time for Eva tomorrow.

E Stuvebod
Stuve-Bodeen, Stephanie.

Mama Elizabeti.